Earth Circles

Written and illustrated by Sandra Ure Griffin

Walker and Company
New York

First published in the United States of America in 1989
by Walker Publishing Company, Inc.

Published simultaneously in Canada by Thomas Allen & Son
Canada, Limited, Markham, Ontario.

Library of Congress Cataloging-in-Publication Data

Griffin, Sandra Ure.
Earth circles/written and illustrated by Sandra Ure Griffin.
p.   cm.
Summary: On the first day of spring a mother and daughter climb a
hill and celebrate the cycles of nature, from the pattern of seed to
flower to the rising and setting of the sun.
ISBN 0-8027-6843-1   ISBN 0-8027-6845-8 (lib. bdg.)

[1. Nature—Fiction.   2. Mothers and daughters—Fiction.]
I. Title
PZ7.G88Ear 1989   [E]—dc19   88-30636

Printed in the United States of America

10 9 8 7 6 5 4 3 2

The artwork was created with a Staedtler Mars 780 mechanical
pencil, applied to Crescent cold press illustration board.
The tonal variations were achieved by carefully varying the
pressure of the pencil's finely-sharpened point.

For my mother, Joan Arden, in loving memory.

"Let's go for a walk," said Mother. "Spring is here and the world is calling. We can climb all the way to the top of the hill and watch the sun set."

"Look," cried Heather. "Today the flowers opened."
"They can feel the Spring," said Mother. "Bend down and listen to their song."

the seeds open and small plants push out and spread slender leaves and grow larger and stronger and bear flowers in Spring and seeds in Summer that drop in Autumn and rest in Winter until the earth warms and... the seeds open and small plants push out and spread slender leaves and grow larger and stronger and bear flowers in Spring and seeds in Summer that drop in Autumn and rest in Winter until the earth warms and...

"Mother," said Heather, "this flower has a butterfly."
"The butterfly has a song, too," said Mother. "Listen to it."

... a caterpillar hatches and eats tender leaves and builds a tight cocoon and hides inside until as a butterfly it spreads its wings and flies to a flower and then beyond to lay its eggs and out of one ...

The butterfly flew over the fence, toward the orchard.
"I see more flowers," said Heather.
"The apple trees have blossomed," said Mother.
"Even the little one I planted," said Heather.
"And all the tall ones too," Mother said, "the ones planted long ago."

...a child digs a hole and buries the roots of a very small tree and waters and watches as it grows taller and one day it flowers and bears fruit for the child and seed for young trees and then...

Heather and her mother followed the fence to the creek.
"The creek looks muddy and deep today," said Heather.
"It rained last night," said Mother. "Listen to the song
of the water."

...the rain falls down to fill the streams and then the sun breaks through spent clouds and under its heat the streams become shallow as new clouds grow large and dark and burdened until they open and...

Across the creek lay the path that led up the hill.
It was a steep climb.
"Can't you carry me?" Heather asked.
"We're almost there," said Mother.

They reached the top.
"Now I can see everywhere!" said
Heather.
"Look across the fields and hills,"
said Mother. "Listen to their song."

Spring throws back Winter's white blanket and the young color warms and spreads and deepens to the rich green of Summer and then it bursts into orange under Autumn's red sun and then all colors disappear until . . .

"I see something past the hills and far away," said
Heather. "What is it, Mother?"
"It's the ocean, Heather. Sit still and close your eyes.
You may hear it calling you."

...the moon pulls the ocean and it slides back from the shore and leaves stones and shells that lie wet on the sand and then the moon lets go and the tide surges back and covers the sand and then...

Heather opened her eyes.
"The sun's going down," she said.
"It's closer to the hills."
"Listen to the falling sun," said Mother.

the sun sinks slowly and colors fade as day turns to night until the sun rises back over the rim of the world and it glows pink and then blazes orange and then soars higher and then soars higher to pour warmth on all below and then...

It grew darker.
"The moon!" said Heather.
"Yes," said Mother.

the moon appears as a silver crescent and each night it swells and grows until a full and shimmering circle fills the night and then the circle dwindles until the last sliver vanishes in the darkness that reigns until ... the moon appears as a silver crescent

"It's late now," Mother said.
"Will you carry me home?" asked Heather.
"I'll carry you," said Mother.

...the sky darkens and the winds blow cool and the child returns home to sleep and dream until the sun calls and the child awakens and rushes out to dance and sing the songs of the day until the light fades away and...

Heather climbed into bed.
"Will you sing me a song?" she asked.
And Mother sang.

one day a baby was born and she grew into a girl and then became a woman who married a man and they created a child who grew within her mother until... grew within her mother until...

...and the mother loved her child and the child grew up and became a mother...